Written by Stephanie Cooke & Insha Fitzpatrick
Art by Juliana Moon

Etch
Houghton Mifflin Harcourt
Boston New York

For all of #TeamNoChill.
Stay weird <3

hmhbooks.com

The text was set in Amescote.

Color by Whitney Cogar
Lettering by Andrea Miller and David Hastings
Edited by Lily Kessinger
Cover and interior design by Andrea Miller

Library of Congress Cataloging-in-Publication Data
Names: Cooke, Stephanie, 1986- author. | Fitzpatrick, Insha, author. | Moon, Juliana, illustrator.
Title: Oh my gods / by Stephanie Cooke & Insha Fitzpatrick ; art by Juliana Moon.
Description: Boston : Houghton Mifflin Harcourt, 2021. | Audience: Ages 10 to 12. | Audience: Grades 4–6. | Summary: When Karen leaves New Jersey to spend time with her enigmatic father on Mount Olympus, she is shocked to learn that her junior high classmates are gods and goddesses, and that one of them is turning people to stone.
Identifiers: LCCN 2019036701 (print) | LCCN 2019036702 (ebook) | ISBN 9780358299516 (hardcover) | ISBN 9780358299523 (trade paperback) | ISBN 9780358296935 (ebook)
Subjects: LCSH: Graphic novels. | CYAC: Graphic novels. | Middle schools—Fiction. | Schools—Fiction. | Fathers and daughters—Fiction. | Zeus (Greek deity)—Fiction. | Gods, Greek—Fiction. | Mythology, Greek—Fiction.
Classification: LCC PZ7.7.C6664 Oh 2021 (print) | LCC PZ7.7.C6664 (ebook) | DDC 741.5/973—dc23
LC record available at https://lccn.loc.gov/2019036701
LC ebook record available at https://lccn.loc.gov/2019036702

Manufactured in China
SCP 10 9 8 7 6 5 4 3 2 1
4500805629

No no no
no no no
no...
Don't do
this to
me!
I need
support!
Jaelle,
quick,
heal me!
WHERE DID
HE COME
FROM?
Ugh, I'm
a goner!

Kaaaaaaaaaaren—
What's up, Mom?!
Can you come down here, please?
Gotta run, talk later!
Good match, everyone!
Coming, Mom!

Hey,
Kare Bear.
Sorry to
interrupt.
Come have a
seat. How was
your game,
sweetie?
It was good. Jaelle still needs help playing support characters, so we went into penalty and got locked out of the next game...
Mom...what's going on?
Mom? Hello? What's up?
Weeeellllll...
I was asked to curate for a huge upcoming gallery show...
...*and* they asked me to contribute a piece to it!
Mom!!!!
That is so amazing. You've worked so hard for this, and you *totally* deserve it.

I didn't even know you were applying for other jobs. I thought you were happy teaching?
Well, that's the thing. I *didn't* apply for the job—they found *me* and asked!
I couldn't believe it. This is my dream job!
When do you start?
Immediately!
Mom, I'm so happy for—
Kare, there's more...
The job isn't exactly, uh, local...
We'll need to shift some stuff around and...I'll have to relocate for a little while...
And...
Mom, what are you saying...
I, umm...
Well, I need you to stay with your father for a bit.

WHAT?!
You want me to go live with Zed?!
I wish you wouldn't call him that... He's still your dad.
But...we barely even see him!
He visits for the holidays!
Yeah, but, like, weird random holidays that no one here has ever heard of!
That's not true! Panathena is a *very big deal* in Greece.
Really, Mom?! Panathena? I don't think that's a big deal *anywhere*...
Kare Bear. I know this is a big adjustment. I just really need this...
I know you don't see your dad a lot, but I thought you'd be happy to get to know each other better...
If you're not okay with it, though, I'll tell the gallery no. You know you come first. You're the most important thing to me.

Okay, fine. I'll go live with Zed.
He's got everything set up for you! The house, a nice private school...
You've given up everything for us. You *do* deserve this.
I'll just really, really miss you...
When do I leave?

ONE WEEK LATER...
NEWARK LIBERTY INTERNATIONAL AIRPORT

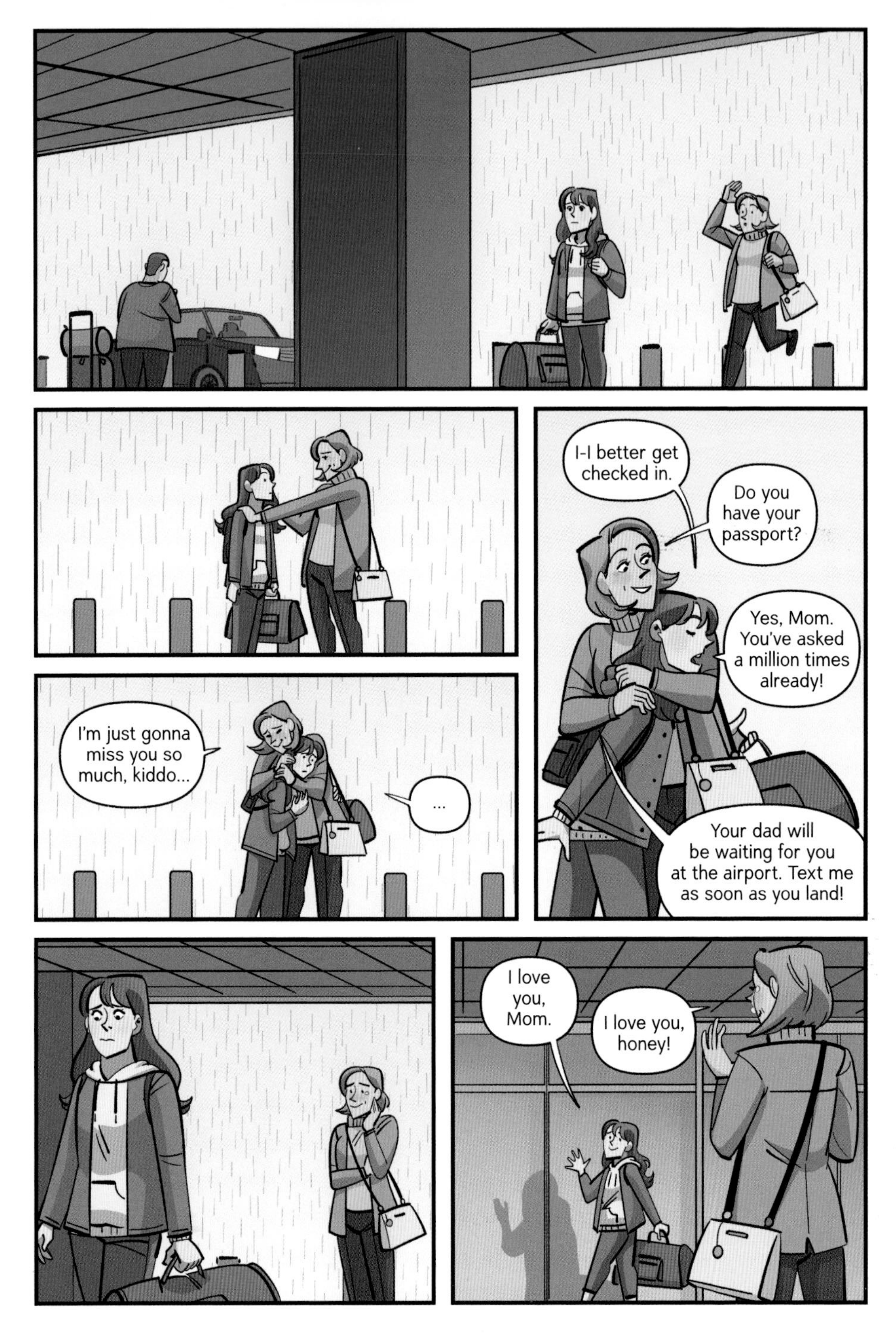
I-I better get checked in.
Do you have your passport?
Yes, Mom. You've asked a million times already!
I'm just gonna miss you so much, kiddo...
...
Your dad will be waiting for you at the airport. Text me as soon as you land!
I love you, Mom.
I love you, honey!

THETA AIR
FLIGHT 1397
PEGAIRSUS
FLIGHT 2030
MT. OLYMPUS
B-14
UP AIRWAYS
FLIGHT 246
MILAN
B-15

Oh dear, you seem to be in the wrong seat!!
You shouldn't be all the way baaaaaaaaah-ck here!
Excuse me? I shouldn't be here—I'm really fine with my other seat—
Nonsense! Only the best for Z—
For, uh, your very first international flight!

Oh, thank you... What is this?
It's sparkling orange juice. And our pleasure! We'll be taking off in a moment. Buckle up.

CLICK

Miss Kaaaaaaren...
Psst... Miss Kaaaren!
Everything okay?
Oh, golly, yes!
I just thought you'd like to get your first look at Mt. Olympus.
Oh, yeah— thank you!

We're here!
It feels so good to be home. You are just gonna love it here, Miss Karen!
I bet...
WELCOME KAREN!!!

KAAAAAAAAREN!
OVER HERE!
Zed! What are you *doing?!*
This is *sooooooo* extra.
Extra-ordinary? Yes, I know! Ha ha!
Give your dad a hug!
Who *are* all these people?
Employees! Colleagues! Friends! They wanted to welcome you to Mt. Olympus!

It's time for some quality time with my daughter, everybody!
You're all dismissed.
Your employees? What do you *do?*
Haven't I told you?
I dabble in a little bit of this and a little bit of that...
But plenty of time to talk about work later, duckling.
We have a chariot to catch.

CHARIOTS
Zeeeeeeeeeeeed, oh my *god.*
...*gods*...
I haven't been obsessed with pegasi for *years* now...
Whatever you paid for these horse costumes is *too much!*
?
?
?
Everyone is going to think I'm some ***spoiled brat...*** *This is so* ***embarrassing.***

Do you want to see your new school?
Zeeeeeed, please just take me home so I don't have to be seen like this...

Are we home?
We are! Come on!
Hurry up! I'll show you around.
Whoa...

Make yourself comfortable. Your rooms are upstairs.
Rooms? I, uh, just need one...
Ah, yes, I sometimes forget how humbly your mother raised you.
Get yourself settled in.
One of the bathrooms is beside your room. Let me know if you require anything.
Let's talk and bond later, daughter!

KAREN'S ROOM

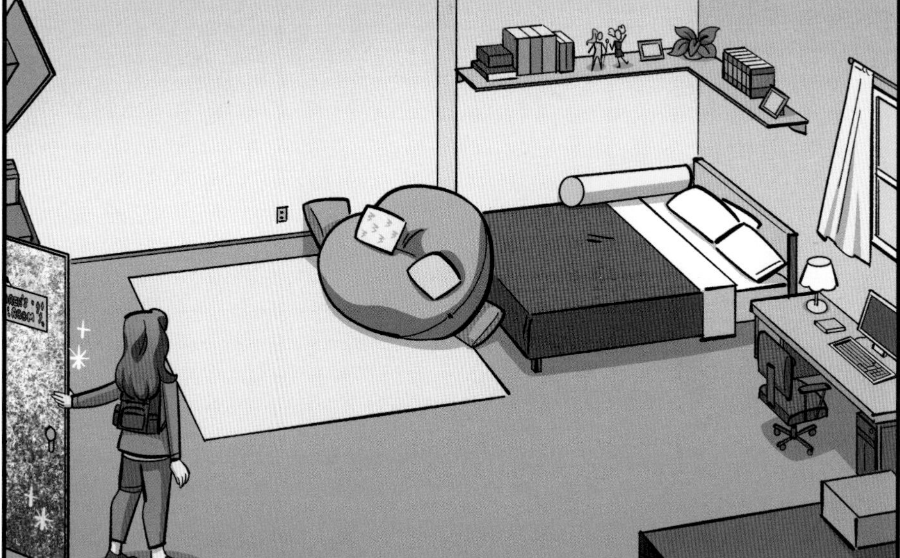

Kare Bear!
Mom! I made it.
Good—I was so anxious—but *how is it so far?!* TELL ME EVERYTHING!
KAAAAREN! Dinner's ready!

I gotta go. Zed has dinner ready.
Kare? Call him Dad, okay? Promise me you'll try...
I know he's a bit...uh, eccentric, but he means well, and he *does* love you.
But not more than I do!
I love you the most. Always.
You don't *always* love me!
Pfft... I don't always *like* you but I will always *love* you.
Okay, give me some love!
Mwah!
That's my girl.
Love youuuuu!
Mwah!
Love you! Have fun with your dad!

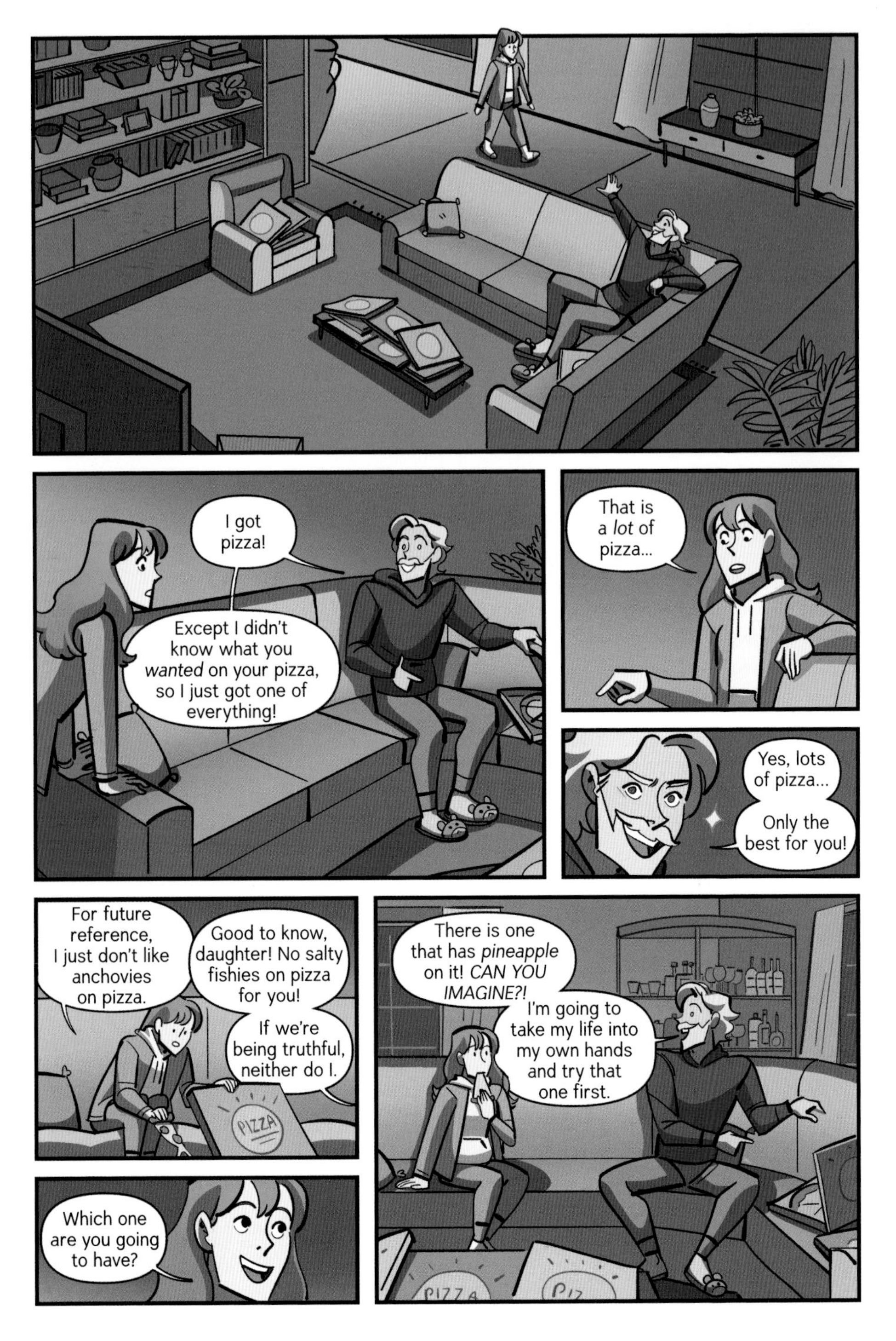
I got pizza!
Except I didn't know what you *wanted* on your pizza, so I just got one of everything!
That is a *lot* of pizza...
Yes, lots of pizza...
Only the best for you!
For future reference, I just don't like anchovies on pizza.
Good to know, daughter! No salty fishies on pizza for you!
If we're being truthful, neither do I.
PIZZA
Which one are you going to have?
There is one that has *pineapple* on it! *CAN YOU IMAGINE?!*
I'm going to take my life into my own hands and try that one first.

Oh! I almost forgot. I picked out a movie for us to watch.
Camila said that you two always have movie nights. So, I thought maybe we could do that too...
Zed—
Err, Dad... this is great.
This is perfect. Honestly. We can do the theater next time.
We can watch it in the theater if you want, or—
OKAY, DAUGHTER!
But we *do* need popcorn once we're done with the pizza.
OH, GOODY!
We should start the film so you can still get to bed early.
Big day tomorrow! You excited for your first day of school?
For sure...

PIZZA

THE NEXT MORNING...

BZZ
BZZ
HAVE THE BEST FIRST DAY OF SCHOOL EVER! THEY'RE ALL GOING TO WANT TO BE FRIENDS WITH YOU AND IF THEY DON'T THEN THEY STINK 💩💩💩

Morning, Dad.
Good morning, daughter!
I read that for important school occasions, young ladies like to get a wrist flower!
So...here!
Uh, well, those are usually for school dances and stuff.
Oh. I see...
Pesky, stupid, confusing mortal traditions...
Okay, fiiiiiine...

Hello, *new girl...*
Sit down, be quiet, and MIND YOUR MANNERS ON THE BUS.
Welcome to the abyss.
What was that?
NOTHING. *TAKE YOUR SEAT.*
Oooookay, then...
LAST STOP.
GET OFF THE BUS.

MT. OLYMPUS JUNIOR HIGH

WHOOSH
GAH!
Hello, m'lady! Welcome to Mt. Olympus Junior High.
I am Hermes, at your service. I'm to be your companion and show you around the ol' campus.
Oh, cool—thanks.
No thanks necessary. It is my duty—nay...*honor*—to assist a goddess as lovely as yourself.
Greeeeaaaat.
WHOOSH
Sorry... I'm really fast.
Riiight...
WHOOSH

The school seems huge at first, but honestly, it's not. We're like one big happy family!
There's only a few places you really need to know about...
CAFETERIA, ADMINISTRATION OFFICE, GYM, POOL, LIBRARY, TRACK, WASHROOMS, THEATER, ASSEMBLY HALL, FIGHTING RING, HOMEROOM, STUDENT LOUNGE, PEGASUS STABLES, THE TEMPLE, GARDENS...
Pegasus stables...?
Let's move on.

This is the administration office.
Good ol' Ms. Hera is the dean's admin assistant. She'll get you your class schedule and can help ya with anything you may need.
Hi—it's my first day...
I know! It's my *business* to know these things...
And the dean informed us of your arrival.
There you go.
Thanks!
Good morning, Dean! Our new student has arrived.
Dad?
"Dad"? No, no... Ha-ha...
I'm the *dean!*
NICE TO MEET YOU, YOUNG LADY.
YOU HAVE A LOVELY WRIST FLOWER!
GOTTA GO!
Shall we carry on?

LUNCHTIME
This is the cafeteria. It's souvlaki day!
Is that a centaur? Wow, someone must be really hot in the back of that costume...
THE TITANS
That's our football team. Big, meaty, full of spirit.
That's the swim team. They're *super* good.
THE SWIM TEAM

THE FATES
THE MYTHBUSTERS
And here are the most beautiful women in the entire scho—
Beat it...
JEFF
Jeff? Wait, who's Jeff?
He's, like, super into pancakes.

And that's the grand tour. It's great, right?
This is *my* crew— we're pretty cool... We saved you a seat.
Uh, well...
Want some fruit?
Well, what do you think so far? Do you love it or do you *love* it?
Well, I... umm...
Excuse me, Hermes. Sorry to interrupt, but Ms. Hera called me over to steal the new girl from you.
You understand. Don't you?
Whatever you want, Dita.
Sigh

Sorry about them. They're a bit...
Eager?
Exactly!
I'm Dita!
I-I'm Karen.
Oh, I like that! Is it short for something?
Nope, just Karen.
Do you know what your next class is?
Uhhh...history. But...shouldn't I be getting to Ms. Hera? You said...
OH! That was just a distraction to get Hermes to stop pestering you!
Can I walk with you to your next class?
Oh, umm... yeah...thank you. Everything here is *super* confusing.
No problem! Don't worry, you'll figure it out quick. Also, I *really* like your hair.
It's beautiful!

So, you just transferred here? Where are you from?
Sorry for all the questions—we don't get new people here very often.
Oh, that's okay. I was living with my mom in New Jersey, but—
Did something happen to your mom?! Is she okay?! Is she sick?! Is she...
No, no, no! Nothing like that. It's just—
She sent me to live with my dad for a bit. She wants me to get to know him...
"Believe in the Fates." That's what everyone says. I mean, they're awful, but ya know?
Uhhh...
They can be really nasty, but everything happens for a reason, right? I met you today, after all!
Here you are! I'll see you around?
Yeah, def!

Ah, the new transfer student. I'm Ms. Clio. Welcome, welcome...
Class, this is, uhhh... Sorry, what's your name, again?
Karen. It's Karen.
Is that short for something?
Not that I know of...
What a bizarre name.
Meet, uh, KAAAAAAARE-EEEN.
Karen. Kare-in.
Sit by Athena. She's our STA* and can help you out.
Scooch along to make room for the new girl, please.
*STA = STUDENT TEACHER ASSISTANT
Uh, hi, nice to meet you, Athena...
You can call me Tina.
Hey, I can help you catch up on lessons, if you want?
Yes, please. This is intense!
Let's meet at the library afterward. It's the building with the huge lion statues in front.
Now that everyone is settled, let's recite all the members of the Grecian oligarchy of 384 BC.

BRRRRNGGG
How is your first day, honey?
WHERE DID U SEND ME? This place is SO FREAKING WEIRD, Mom.
That bad, huh? Is your father okay, at least? Is he feeding you?
SURE, MOM, EVERYTHING IS GREAT.
THUD
Oh no. Oh no. I'm sorry 'bout that! You okay?
You mean, in general? Thaaat's up in the air...
Long day?
The *longest*.

I'm Karen and I gotta run...
Which direction is the gym?
I'm Pol. Well, Apollo, but... yeah, just call me Pol.
You've got PE?
Yeah, why? Is it bad?!
Well, the upside is that my sister also has PE this period. You'll be okay.
Her name's Artemis.
Oh, what's she look like?
Trust me. She stands out...
She's not great with people, but I'll put in a good word for you!
Thank you! That's so nice of you...

The gym is down that way. Can't miss it. You'll see a couple of gigantic Spartan statues at the sides of the doors.
Thanks!
WAIT!
You dropped this. Sorry again...
I can't believe I almost left it behind. My *whole life* is on here... THANK YOU!

They are **super** committed to the theater here. They're so **method**...
Wow, you really can't miss these statues...

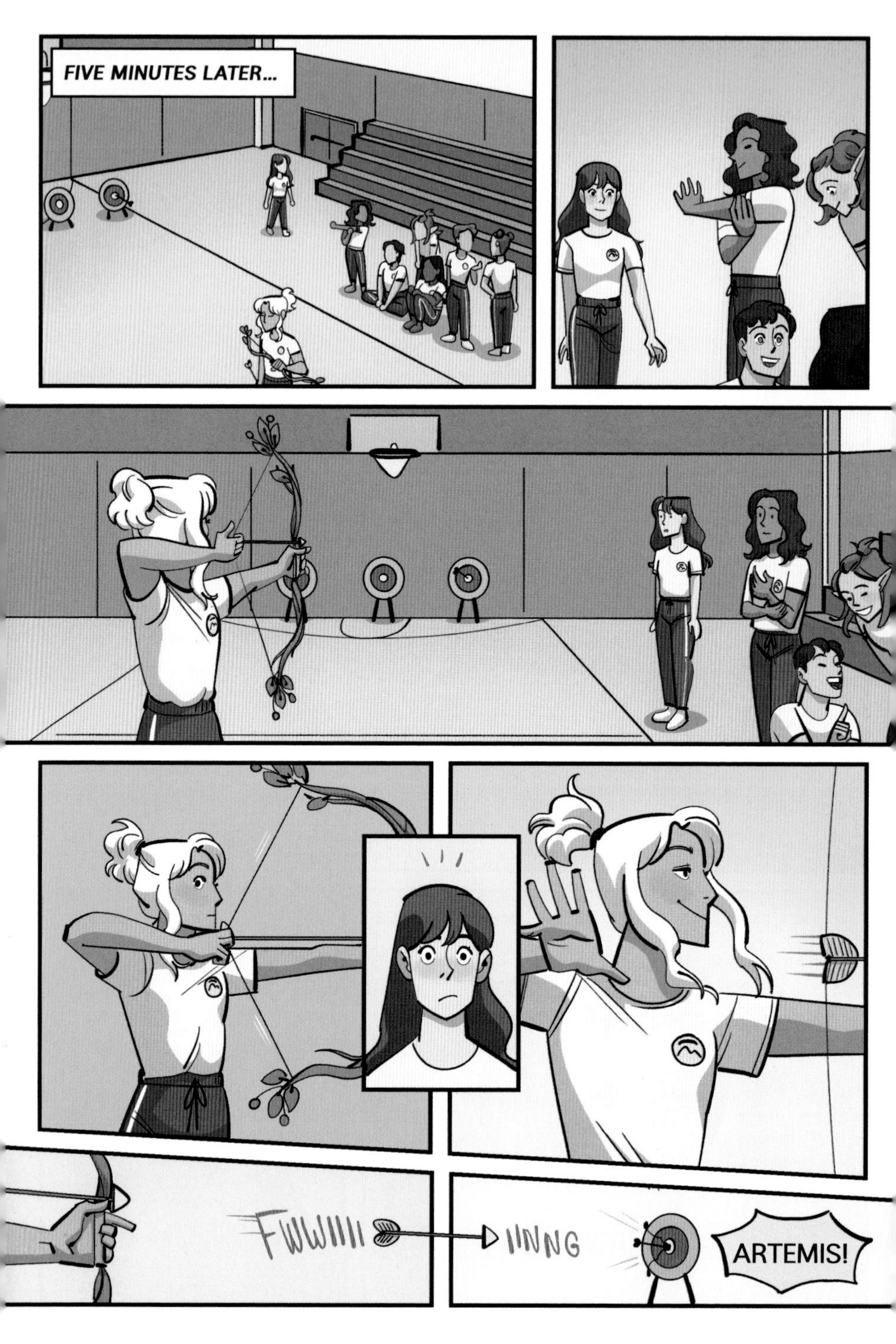
FIVE MINUTES LATER...
FWWIIII
IINNG
ARTEMIS!

What have I told you about splitting school arrows?
We do not have the budget to constantly buy new arrows to replace the ones you destroy!
Whoooaaaa...
HEY!
What do you think you're doing?!

You can't just go around touching other people's bows!
I'm, uh, sorry...
You *should* be sorry!
This bow is one of a kind and was custom made for *me*.
No one else touches it...

Hmmm...
But she... Ugh...
You must be Karen...
How'd you—
My brother says you're new...
Your brother?
I'm Artemis.
Ohh! You're Pol's sister!
It's nice to meet you.
You're welcome.
Listen, Pol says you seem cool. So, I'm going to cut you some slack.
But never touch my bow. Got it?
? ?

Of course...
I really didn't mean anything by it, honest...
FWIING
Big yikes...

ONE PAINFULLY LONG PE CLASS LATER...
Gosh, you look tired.
Thanks...

BOOMPH

I am *so* sorry...
I keep running into people today...

Whoa...you have really pretty eyes!
How...
Anyways, sorry again— I have to get going.
See ya, green!
She... can look at me...

Sorry I'm late!
SHHHHHHHHHHHHHH!
Sorry!
MISS POLYHYMNIA
Thanks for helping me out.
It's no biggie. Take a seat!

TUESDAY
WEDNESDAY
THURSDAY
FRIDAY

MONDAY
...and that's why Alexander is considered to be one of the greatest military commanders in history.
I know it's a *lot* to get caught up on, but you've been doing great!
The curriculum here is *so* weird. At my old school, we just learned about Abraham Lincoln.
Abra-who?
Let's call it a night?
Yes, please. My brain can't absorb any more, especially on a Monday!
So, how are you liking it here so far?
It's just...very, very, very...
...different.
I get that.
But I'm glad you're here! It's really nice to have a new friend.

AAAAAAAHHHHH!!
What was that?!
Hello?
Are you all right?
We should make sure everything is okay.
Umm...

Hello?
Are you okay?

Is that...?

We have to call the Higher Authorities.
The what?!
The Higher Authorities! Our local law enforcement.
The police.
This is, like, straight out of Greek mythology.
Is this some sort of prank?
Umm...
Let's go...

6:00 P.M.

I'm Officer Soter. You must be Karen and Athena.
I know you've already given your statements, but I wanted to ask one more time if you saw anything else.
Sometimes even the smallest detail can turn out to be very helpful.
Before we found the... the...
The student?
Yeah... Well, I thought I saw something.
Someone ran out from the other end of the bookshelves. Toward the door.

Could you describe them?
No... Sorry.
I thought I was just seeing things until we found...
Thank you, Karen. I think we can call it a night. Let's get you packed up to go home, okay?
NOD
ZIP
?

Sorry—I think I left my phone by the table. One sec!
I haven't seen anything like this in a *long* while.
Didn't we find something like this on the outskirts of town a few years back?
Yep...
My gods. Hopefully we'll find the culprit soon.

So, I know it's been a weird night...
That's a huge understatement to how weird this night has been!
Ha, yeah, but if you want to relax for a bit, I'm meeting up with my friends at Ambrosia. Wanna come with?
I'm not sure. I don't want to crash your hangout.
It'll be good to take your mind off everything.
Plus, I think you'll get along with my friends.
I think you met Dita last week during lunch.
Okay! If you think it'll be fine.
NOD
It will!

AMBROSIA
AMBROSIA
OPEN

OMGs, hiiiiiii!
I see you've already met everyone.
Hello again. Tina let me tag along—I hope that's okay. This place is really chill.
Did you want to borrow a sweater?
Whaa? Uh, no, no. Chill, like—
The usual?
YEP!
You got it, babes—
Oh, look at this new face! Do you want a menu, sweetie?
She doesn't need one—she'll have what we're having.
Trust me.

What in the River Styx took you so long?
Thank you, Ambrosia!
Well...you know I've been helping tutor Karen.
We were in the library and...a student was turned to stone.

A student? Turned to stone?
Are you sure it wasn't some weird prank?
I'm sure...
The Higher Authorities came and took statements from us.
I don't understand how this is happening...
I thought I saw someone leave the library after it happened, but I didn't get a good look.
So...
There was someone in the library with you who was turned to stone...
Right...
Refresh my memory, *new girl*... How long have *you* been here?

Are you implying—
You can't be serious!
How would *I* be turning people to *stone?!* How could anyone?
You don't think it's a weird coincidence that you arrived at Mt. Olympus and then *all of this* starts happening?
Be reasonable, Artemis!
She was with me the whole time!
And she didn't once get up to use the bathroom?
Well...

That's *enough!*
We need to remember to love and be compassionate.
Karen is new here, and sure, it's a *big* coincidence, but *our Tina* is saying she didn't do it.
Art, you may not trust Karen yet, but you trust Tina... right?
I guess...
Good! Now, let's move past this, okay?
Fiiiiine...
Karen said she saw someone or some*thing*, so...
Maybe we should think about alternate suspects!

A GUIDE TO MONSTERS & MYTHOLOGICAL CREATURES
PLOF
Do they not know about Google here...
A GUIDE TO MONSTERS & MYTHOLOGICAL CREATURES
Maybe we can find something in my book that will help jog your memory about what you saw!
In *this* book?

HYDRA
Nah...
No one's seen a Chimera for ages...
CHIMERA
Not unless Cyclopes have suddenly developed powers besides being big and clueless...
Maybe, but I've never heard of one turning someone to stone before.
KOBALOS
A unicorn?
Everyone's a suspect, Dita.

Do any of these seem familiar? I mean, it doesn't seem likely, but—
UNICORN
What, monsters?!
You *guys!*
This is bonkers...
Monsters aren't *real.*
Okay, fine. I'll play along. It *sounds* like a Gorgon to me, but—
A Gorgon would make perfect sense!
But there haven't been any Gorgons around for millennia...
Are you even *hearing* yourself?! Are you guys in on this? I'm being pranked, right? Monsters? Unicorns? *GORGONS?!*
Why is everyone here *so dramatic?* This fancy-arts-school thing has *really* gotten to you all...
?
?
?
?

Ha ha ha ha ha...

Umm... Karen...
Nope.
Karen...
Nope!
Karen.... monsters...
MONSTERS AREN'T REAL!
You've really got your tutoring work cut out for you, Tina...
You live in Mt. Olympus.
The Mt. Olympus...
Okay, and...?!

In New Jersey, did you study mythology in school?
Pfft—of *course* we did!
I mean, I know *all about* Mt. Olympus and the gods and goddesses, but, like, none of that's *true*...
My friend's mom told me that myths are based in *some* truth, but...
Wait—
Are you all in some kind of weird mythology-worshiping LARPing group?!
Seriously?!
GAH!
Yikes...
OMGs...
So...
I'll take that as a no?

Remember when we met? I told you my name is Apollo, but I go by Pol?
Yeah! Like Apollo Creed from the Rocky movies!
More like Apollo, god of the sun...
And music!
My name is *Athena!*
Goddess of wisdom.
And justice!
I'm Aphrodite—
Goddess of love and beauty.

And I'm Artemis...
Goddess of the—
What the heck is all this?
NOPE! STOP IT!
Goddess of the moon and the hunt.

. . .
Let's say that I *believe* you...
How would that even *work?!* Greek gods and goddesses have been around for at least a thousand years.
You're all *my* age!
Immortality is boring...
Some of us choose to be reborn and grow up in new generations.
It keeps things fun!
And it's easier to adjust to the world with fresh minds.
Then how am *I* here?!
Isn't Mt. Olympus supposed to *only* be for gods and goddesses?

Well, yeah.
Didn't you know? Everyone's at least *some* form of god, goddess, or "mythological" creature here.
How am *I* here, then?!
There's only one way you *could* be here...
What? What does that *mean?*
Umm...
It means that you have to at *least* be a demigoddess.
I can't believe your dad didn't tell you...
A...
...demigoddess?!

Demigoddess...

Karen?
Karen...?
KAREN!
HA
HA
HA
HA
We should call it a night. It's been a long day.
Yeah, that's a good idea.
I—I need to talk to my dad.

See you tomorrow!
SMK
Is Mt. Olympus that different from home?

Ha ha ha
ha ha ha
ha ha ha
ha ha!
Oh, right.
You're serious.
Yeah. It is.
It's hard being away
from everyone. I really
miss my mom and my
friends.
UGH
I know we can't
replace your friends back
home, but for what it's worth,
I hope we can be
your friends.
GRUMBLE
GRUMBLE
GRUMBLE
I'm pretty sure
she doesn't want
that at all.
Artemis?
She'll come around.
She's a big softy at heart,
aren't you, Art?

You really have had the longest first week...
Seriously.
I should get home. My dad has some explaining to do.

See you tomorrow?
See you tomorrow.

Umm, guys? Ha-ha... So yeah, funny story. I don't know where I live? How do I get to 3 Oak Street?

We'll walk you home.

MEANWHILE...

SNIFF
SNIFF

SNIFF
SNIFF

We told you not to go outside. We told you this would happen!
I didn't mean to hurt anyone... There was a girl! She could look at me, a-and...
The only people you ever need are us, your sisters. The sooner you learn that, the better.
Look at what your carelessness has done already!
I DIDN'T MEAN TO!
Where are you going?! You can't go back out there!

MEDUSA!!!

Daughter, what are you doing with your cereal?
I'm not really hungry...
Breakfast is the most important meal of the day! You must eat!
!

I didn't know you took breakfast so seriously.
Everyone should take breakfast seriously, daughter.
Is everything all right?
Yes...
No...
Ugh...
Dad, can I ask you something?
Anything, daughter.
Am I a demigoddess?
What?! You? A *demigoddess?* Like in Greek mythology? You?! Who put these ideas in your head?
. . .
I knew we'd have to have this talk eventually...
Yes... You are a demigoddess.
Oh my god—
Gods. Plural.

So. That would make you a *god?!*
NOD
. . .
Who are you *really?*
Come with me, daughter.

Wait there, daughter.
CRAAACK
WAHHH!

Daughter, are you okay?
I...
You're...
The lightning...
Does *Mom* know about this?!
Well...umm... uhhh... not exactly.
What do you mean "not exactly"?
It's... a complicated situation...
So, do you, like, run Mt. Olympus, then?!
I am the mayor!
And the dean?
I... Yes... I am also the dean...
Why did you pretend to not know who I was at school, then?!
I just... I didn't want...

I didn't want you to think differently of me.
I wanted you to get to know the *real* me. Zed. Dad. *Your* dad.
Do I have, like...
...powers?!
Uhhh...
Well...
We don't really know yet...
Part of the reason I wanted you to come stay with me was to keep an eye on you as you hit puber—
We do *not* need to have *that* talk...
Trust me, Mom has already filled me in.
But I *might* have powers?

Could I have the power to...
...turn someone to stone?
Is this about yesterday at school?
Maybe...
Hmmm...
Maybe?
We do not always understand the powers that are given to us, and they have taken many forms over the years.
It is impossible to rule out the possibility, daughter...
Right. Well, I should probably get to school.
Do you want a ride? We can take the chariot!!
Uh, no thanks. I think I can find my way.
All right, love bug! Off you go.

CAFETERIA
LATER...
surf

THUD

Karen, what are you doing?!
I want to clear my name.
What do you mean?!

I've been thinking about last night...

Artemis was right.
Excuse me?!
This body turns up around the same time that I arrive in Mt. Olympus...
If Artemis put that together, the...the, uhhh...
Higher Authorities?
Yeah, them! Well, they've probably put that together too.
I want to clear my name.

I'm in.
I can respect that you want to take action. Gotta admit, it's a bold move.
I'm in too.
Of course I'll help.
Me too!

So, what's the plan?
Plan?
Uh, well, umm...
Who needs a plan when you've got the goddess of wisdom and strategy on your side?
You don't have a *plan?!*
We *need* a plan...
THUD

Tina, take a deep breath. We'll think of something together.
If there hasn't been a Gorgon spotted in Mt. Olympus for millennia, there *definitely* isn't one enrolled at school.
Still, the signs *do* point to a Gorgon.
And it's *very* strange that someone was turned to stone here at the school...
We could check the Mt. Olympus census against the list of students enrolled at school!

How would that help?
We can see if anyone our age is missing and not accounted for.
How are we going to do that?
Like, how are we going to get the census *and* the student list?
What do you mean?
As an STA, I have access to the admin office. We can just *borrow* the records for a bit.
Right. To get the records, won't we have to go to city hall?
Because the school dean is *also* the mayor!
...who is also the mayor.
But...the dean...is my dad...
Well, he keeps all the records here.
Okay, so what do we do?
The dean goes for a walk after he eats his lunch. If we're fast, we may be able to catch the window now. Here's the plan...

STEP ONE: CREATE A DIVERSION

A FEW MINUTES LATER...
I can't take it anymore...
Is there something I can help you with?
I can't take it. It's just *so* much...
Is everything okay...?
No, everything is *not* okay!
What seems to be the issue?
Where do I even *begin?!*

STEP TWO: SET UP A LOOKOUT
Remember the signal, Tina.
We'll make an owl call if there's danger...
WHOOO! WHOOOOOO!
TEE HEE

GO TITANS
STEP THREE: SNEAK INTO THE DEAN'S OFFICE
I'm new here and I hardly know *anyone*...
I miss my friends back home and my *mom.*
And my *totally normal school.*
Mt. Olympus is, like, *so* weird and...
CLICK

STEP FOUR: FIND STUDENT RECORDS AND CENSUS
Psst... Tina!
What are you *doing?!*
Whoa...
You need to keep distracting Ms. Hera!
Oh, she's gone. She said she needed to excuse herself to take care of some urgent business elsewhere that suddenly came up.
She's not much of a people person...
What *is* all of this?
It's the dean's office *and* the mayor's office.

Where does *that* lead?
City hall. The office is enchanted to be in two places at once to optimize the dean/mayor's days.
We need to get to work. Ms. Hera will be back soon.
You look for the town census over there. I'll get the student records.
Got them!
I don't even know what I'm looking for...
Never mind—found it!
CURRENT MT. OLYMPUS CENSUS RECORDS

CURRENT MT. OLYMPUS CENSUS RECORDS
THUNK
I wonder if we can copy these by Ms. Hera's desk...
No need! I'll just take pictures.
What is *that?* Your phone is so big!
Ours are far more compact.
Is that a flip phone?! I think my mom used to have one of those...

Whoooaaaa!
You should upgrade your phone!
I *just* got the latest model available here.
Oh.
FLIP
Old things are in! I bet a group of hipsters in New York would kill for your phone model.
What are "hipsters"?
Oh, Tina. I have so much to show you. I'll tell you later.
We should finish taking photos of everything.

Why are there *so many* student records...
At least the census wasn't so ba—
WHOOO! WHOOOOOO!
THE SIGNAL!
What are we going to do?!
We gotta move quick!

Tina and Karen are still in there!
Go. Get them out of there.

WHOOSH
Oh, thank gods it's just you...
We gotta get out of here! The dean is coming down the hall.
We heard the signal!
Then let's go!
We're almost done!
Artemis can only hold him off for so long.

Artemis. Good to see you.
What are you doing in the hallway with your bow?
I, uhhh...
Target practice!
Target practice? Here?
YEP. The archery course wasn't doing it for me, so I thought I'd practice in here a bit...
You *what?!*
You should walk me right to detention!
I don't see any targets...
Uhhh...

Did you just shoot an arrow down the hall?!?!
At a fellow *student?!*
Umm...
That was...

...AWESOME!
I mean, that shot was just *bananas!*
A *bananas* shot at an *apple!*
IT WAS APPLES!
HA HA HA... *APPLES*...
HIGH FIVE!
What a good shot that was...
WOWWWWIIIIEEEE!

WHOOOOOO!
WHOOOOOOOOOO!
You guys!
The dean is coming and we have to go!
NOW!
Come on, Karen. We have to get out of here.
Just a sec...
What are we going to do with all these papers?!
Just leave them!
Hmmm...
I swore I closed this door...

Huh...
I guess I shouldn't have left that window open.

OOF!
UGH...

We did *not* see this coming...
Well, well...
If it isn't the bookworm and the bohemian bottom feeder herself. Where's that music maestro of yours?
Uhhh...
That was rhetorical. We don't care...
Not about you or your missing musical maven.
You, on the other hand...
You're *very* interesting, new girl...
PAT PAT
Are you done yet? We have things to do, places to go, people to—

Her future...
We can't see it clearly...
It's *clouded*...
What *are* you?
Come on, Atropos. Let's get out of here.

What's their deal?
The Fates? Let's just say that you don't want to get on their bad side.
They seem...
Nice?
Ha-ha! Yeah, *that's* the word for—
AHHHHHHHHHHHHHH!
What is it?

You've found your musical maven...
Pol...
At least we know it wasn't Karen...
We need to find whoever did this *now*...

THUD
Ha ha!
Can we play hide-and-seek now?
Hmmm...
Ooookay, but don't wander too far away.
You're the best, Eury!

Eury, you count first! Stheno and me will hide.
You mean "Stheno and I."
Yeah! Don't forget to start counting!
1...2...3... 4...5...
...6...7...8... 9...10...

Ready or not, here I come!
HEE HEE
RUFF RUFF
Eep!
RUFF
Oh, hello!

You wanna play with us too?!
RUFF!

AAAAAHHHHHHHHHHHHHHHH!

What happened?!
HELP HIM!
We have to *help him!*
We *can't,* Medusa.
This can't be *undone...*
Eury, please... We have to. We *have* to.
He was trying to play with me and—

We have to go, Medusa. We can't let anyone see.
We have to hide him before anyone finds him.
Eury, we *can't*!
We can help him! He'll be okay! Right?
We can't leave him!
We *have to*!
Do you *want* to be taken away from us?
Do you want that?!
Noooo...
SNIFF SNIFF
Help us move him, then. Come on.

Medusa. This is a lesson for you.
People will always fear us because of *that*. We will *always* be monsters to them.
You can't forget who and *what* you are.

We're your family *and* your friends.
That's how it *has* to be. No one can know about us.
We'll never be understood.
You can *never* be friends with others. They'll hurt you. They'll take you away...
You'll be without us. Your only family. Your only friends.
I don't believe you...
What?
I DON'T BELIEVE YOU!
Medusa, you—
I didn't *mean* to hurt him...

You'll see! Someday I'll leave the lighthouse. I'll live like everyone else.

LIBRARY
LATER...
Please tell me you found something...
We *have* to find who did this to Pol.
We found something...
Karen and I compared the census and student records.
There were three anomalies.
NAME: Grææ, Euryale
CLASSIFICATION: Kobaloi
AGE: 24
ADDRESS: 175 Alexandria Point
NAME OF MOTHER: Grææ, Ceto
NAME OF FATHER: Grææ, Phorcys
ADDITIONAL FAMILY: Grææ, Stheno, & Grææ, Medusa
AFFILIATED ORGANIZATIONS (SCHOOL, WORK, ETC.): N/A
HIGHEST LEVEL OF EDUCATION COMPLETED: N/A–homeschooled
AME: Grææ, Stheno
LASSIFICATION: Kobaloi
GE: 20
DDRESS: 175 Alexandria Point
NAME OF MOTHER: Grææ, Ceto
NAME OF FATHER: Grææ, Phorcys
ADDITIONAL FAMILY: Grææ, Euryale, & Grææ, Medusa
AFFILIATED ORGANIZATIONS (SCHOOL, WORK, ETC.): N/A
HIGHEST LEVEL OF EDUCATION COMPLETED: N/A–homeschooled
NAME: Grææ, Medusa
CLASSIFICATION: Kobaloi
AGE: 13
ADDRESS: 175 Alexandria Point
NAME OF MOTHER: Grææ, Ceto
NAME OF FATHER: Grææ, Phorcys
ADDITIONAL FAMILY: Grææ, Stheno, & Grææ, Euryale
AFFILIATED ORGANIZATIONS (SCHOOL, WORK, ETC.): N/A
HIGHEST LEVEL OF EDUCATION COMPLETED: N/A–homeschooled

Anomalies?
This family is classified on the census as kobaloi, but everyone knows they're extinct.
What are kobaloi?
A kobalos is a nasty gnome-like creature. A little trickster.
So, you don't think they're behind this?
I don't know. This feels *off.*
We should follow this lead. I think it's time to investigate.
Okay— where to?
According to this, they live in that lighthouse on the outskirts of town.
I was always told not to go there...
Why don't we start there?

The lighthouse?
Yeah, by Lake Olympus.
There's a lake?
This is Mt. Olympus... *all* of it.

MT. OLYMPUS.
Here, let me show you...
Oops, other side.
LAKE OLYMPUS
LIGHTHOUSE
DOWNTOWN
SUBURBS
AIRPORT
Here! Take a look.

Mt. Olympus is a lot bigger than I thought...
Did your dad not show you around or anything?
Weeeell, he *tried* to show me around, but I wasn't really paying attention...
So, we think the culprit may be at the lighthouse?
It's looked abandoned for a while now, but we can go there to see if we can find some clues.
We should get going.
We still have lots of daylight left since school was let out early.

We should get prepared, just in case.
Let's stop by my place first.
Good idea.
Lead the way!
Where are you kids off to?
Oh, uh, hey!
Hello, student to whom I shall not show any direct favoritism.
Right. Well, we're just off to study...umm—
Nature!
Yep, we're going to study nature for a project! On the outskirts of town at the lighthouse.
WHAT EXCELLENT STUDENTS YOU ARE.
Well, good for you all.
Just be careful out there!
I don't want more students getting turned to stone!

ARTEMIS & POL'S HOUSE

Whoooaaa, cool tree house.
She built it by herself for her and Pol.

She built the shed herself, too.
That's *so* cool...

Let's gear up.

A FEW MINUTES LATER...
The pen is mightier than the sword!
Hmmm... Well, how about if you just had an *actual* sword.
Okay, *fiiiiiiine.*
I don't think I should have this...
I have *no idea* how to use it. Or what we're about to do.
It's easy. I'll give you a quick lesson...

What, now?
Follow my lead.
Okay!
Hold your stance like this and your bow like this...
Practice pulling back the bowstring to get a feel for it.
It'll strain, but pull it toward you slowly and hold on tight.
Now we're going to nock and loose an arrow.

Nock the arrow like this...
Take aim...
THWP
Fire.
Come on, you got this. Hold it steady...
Aim.
Fire.

Ahhhhhh! I'm sorry!
I'll be taking *that* back now...
Sorry!
So, what should I take, then?
You...
You can just stand behind us.
That's fair...
Not bad for your first try.

We should get going.
Let's go find whoever's doing this...
And save Pol.

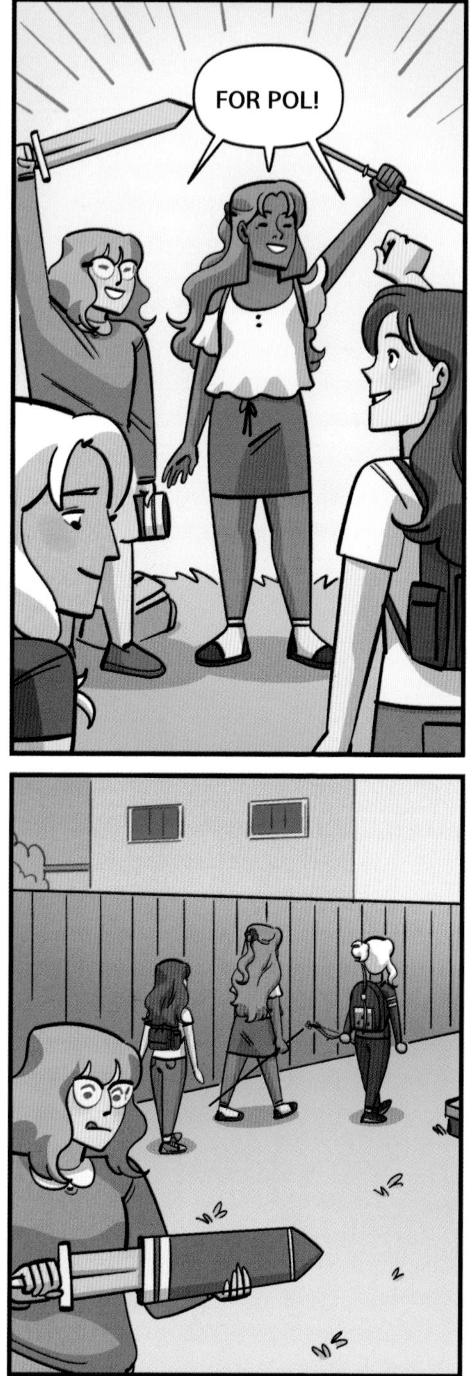
FOR POL!

Quit dawdling, Karen!

This is it?
Yep!
Let's take a look around.
But be on the lookout for danger.
We don't know who...or *what*... is here.
Dita, you're with me.
Karen and Artemis, you two pair up.
NOD
NOD
We watch each other's backs. Okay?
We'll check around back there.
You check around the garage.
Remember the signal.
WHOOO! WHOOOOOO!

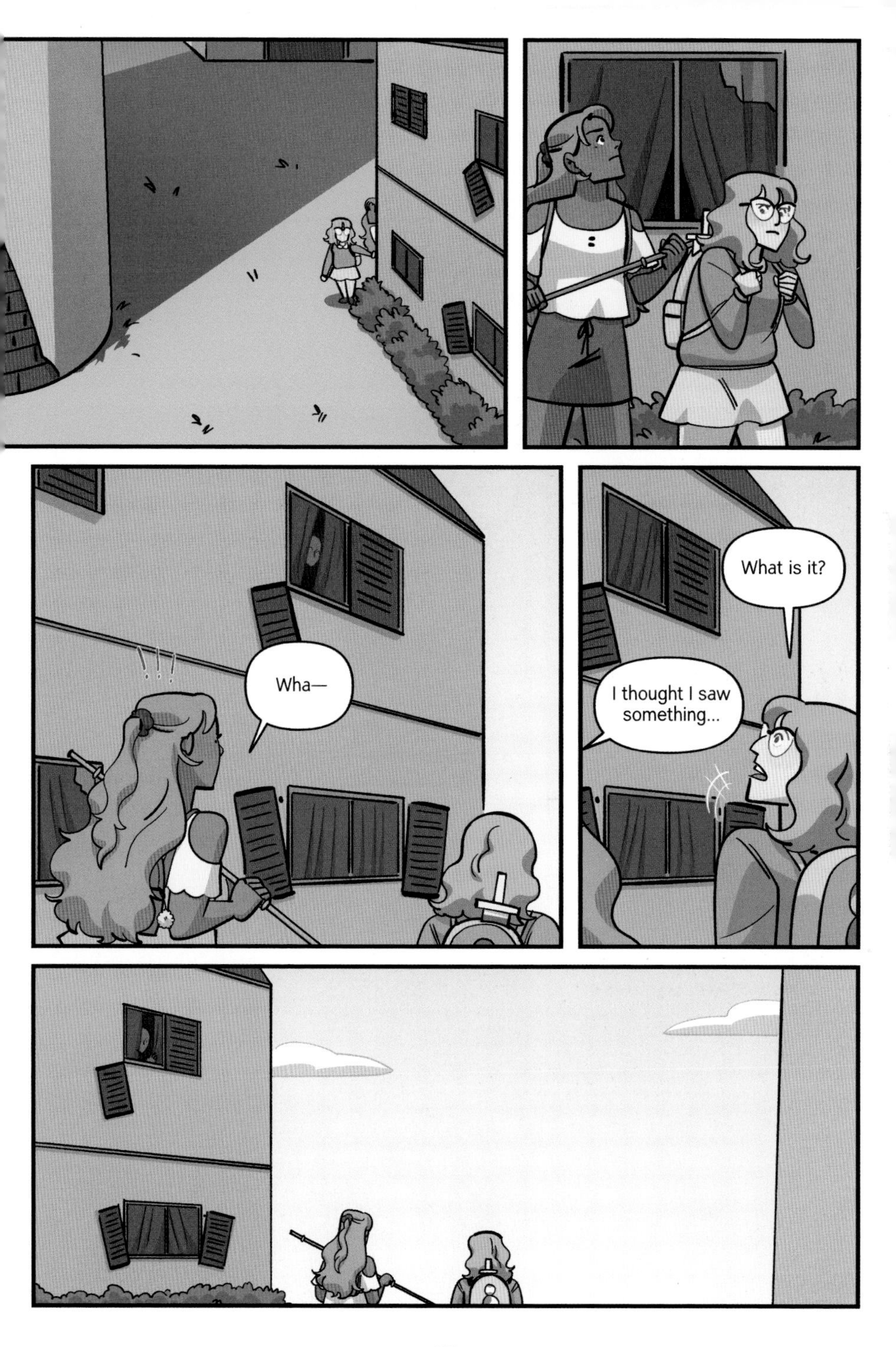
!!!
Wha—
What is it?
I thought I saw something...

Whose stupid idea was it to find the baddies turning people to stone?!
You. It was your idea.
Right...
We should check it out.
I don't know about this—
No one's lived here in ages— it'll be fine.
Okaaaaaaay.
WHOOSH

What the heck—
Whoooaaa...

Tina! Dita! We found something...
WHOOO! WHOOOOOO!
Let's go!
Hello, *trespassers*...

Do you think they're okay?
They should've found us by now...
I'm not sure...
I'm going to go find them.
I can come with...
No, no. What if they come back? You'll be fine. Stay here and wait.
If I'm not back in five minutes, come find me. Okay?
Uh, okay...
It's *you!* You came to see me...
Wahhhh!

Who's there...
What do you want?
We can be *real* friends now!
Friends?
Who *are* you?
Oh! I'm so sorry! How silly of me...
When you're stuck at home as much as I am, you sometimes forget your manners.
I'm Medusa!
M-M-Medusa?!
That's me! And you're Karen, right?
Umm, yeah! Hi.
What are you doing out here? Why are you turning people to stone?

You... You're a Gorgon?!
Yeah. And?
You... You're the one turning people to stone!
What? What are you talking about? We live out here and keep to ourselves. We mind our own business...
Unlike some people...
Whatever you do, don't look them in the eyes!
That's not what your garage full of stone bodies tells us...
It's unfortunate that you saw that...
Now you'll understand why we can't let you leave...
We don't want to hurt you!
Your kind *always* wants to hurt us...
We really don't want to cause any trouble.
We're just trying to help our friend.
ARGHHHHHHHHHHH!

How do you know my name?
I've been following you... ever since the day we met.
You're *different* from the others...
You're not affected by...
You told me I had pretty eyes...
No one's ever said that to me before...
You're the girl I ran into in the hall...
Whoa...
When we ran into each other, I expected the worst to happen...

I am *so* sorry...
I keep running into people today...
I thought I would hurt you, too...
But you looked right at me and saw me. No one has ever done that before...
Whoa...you have *really* pretty eyes!
Besides my sisters...
Then you left before I could say anything...
Anyways, sorry again—I have to get going.
See ya, green!
I don't have much experience making friends...
So, I followed you and tried to work up the nerve to talk to you...

TUESDAY
I didn't work up the nerve that day...
WEDNESDAY
So, I kept trying...
THURSDAY
And trying...
FRIDAY
And trying...

Don't be stupid. Just go talk to her...
MONDAY
Hi, I'm Medusa...
No, that's stupid...
Hey, it's you! We met the other day?
I'm "Green," remember? But my real name is Medusa...
Ugh, that's even *worse*...
Stupid, stupid, stupid...
Are you okay?

AHHHHHHHHHHHHHH HHHHHHHHHHHHHH!!!!
What was that?!
Oh no. No, no, no, no, no...
This can't be happening...
We should make sure everything is okay.
Umm...
Hello? Are you all right?
I've gotta get out of here...
??

You were *following* me...
I-I'm really sorry. I never meant to hurt anyone...
I just wanted to be your friend.
I get it.
The loneliness, that is. Not the whole turning-people-to-stone part...
I'm an only child, and my mom works a lot. I spend a lot of time by myself.
I've felt different all my life.
Now I find out my dad's not who I thought he was. *I'm* not who I thought I was.
It's scary. The scariest thing in the world is being different. But sometimes...it's pretty great. I'm learning that the hard way.
ARGHHHHHHHHHHHH!
Artemis!
Oh no— my sisters!

Get off me!
Eury!
Don't hurt them!
They— can't— leave...
They've—seen— too—much...
It's my fault!
What do you mean...
I-I-I, umm...
I've been sneaking into town...
I wanted to make friends, and I bumped into Karen...
She was kind to me...
I tried to talk to her... I wanted to introduce myself, and I—
I accidentally turned some people to stone...
I'm to blame for all of this...

Medusa—
We've talked about this *over* and *over* again.
How could you have been so—
There!

Wha—

I may regret this, but—
Look at me.
But... I might...
Trust me. That's what friends do.

I can see you! I can see you!
Whoa there...
You still have to be careful.
Eury, I can see! I'm not hurting anyone!
What is going on?!
Who are you people?
Stheno, I can look at them!

How did you know that would work?
I, uhhh...well, I wasn't totally sure that it would.
I was able to make eye contact with her in the hall before, so I just hoped it would cancel out her stare now.
KAREN!
Well, that was good thinking.
Really, really good thinking...
Why didn't I think of that?
Eury, we have to call the Higher Authorities. We have to—
I know... I know... We have to make things right... I know.
I'll go inside and make the call.

A LITTLE WHILE LATER...
It says here on your papers that you're, uh, a family of kobaloi.
That's clearly not the case. As such, you're a family of unregistered Class 5 mythos.
You must understand how this looks...
It's my fault, sir. I tried to keep us confined to the lighthouse, but my sister— she's just a kid.
She didn't know better. She doesn't understand her powers yet...
I'm so sorry. I knew what could happen if I went outside...
I just wanted to have a normal life, make friends...

They're not evil. They were protecting themselves.
It was an *accident.*
Those look like a *lot* of accidents...
Oof...
Yeah...that looks bad, real bad, but Medusa can't control it.
She didn't go out with the *intent* to hurt anyone!
Please. She's my friend.

Sheriff, surely we can work something out.
Have a little compassion...
Well...
We could—
I THINK WE'VE FIGURED IT OUT! We know what to do!
I was looking at the people turned to stone and thinking about the way that it all happened. We need to take some samples from Medusa and her sisters, but I think a component in their DNA holds the key to reversing it!
But what does that *mean*, Tina?
It means we can change everyone back. Including Pol!

Really? You swear it will work?
Yes! I think so.
Art, you're hurting me...
Oh. Sorry.
If everything that Medusa has done is undoable, we can find a way to go easy on her.
Hasn't she suffered enough in isolation?
Thinking that she would never have friends her *whole life?!*

It's not safe here yet, Mr. Mayor!
You should get back to city hall...
I heard my daughter's name on the dispatch. I have to find her!
Where's my daughter?!
Dad?
DAUGHTER!!!

Dad!
Dad, I haven't asked you for a lot... but I'm asking for something now.
Please find a way to help Medusa and her sisters.
Well, my little snickerdoodle, she turned a *bunch* of people to stone...
By *accident!*
Accident or not, it's still a pretty big deal.
What if I, like, vouched for her? I can help keep an eye on her until she figures out her powers.

Hmmm... I don't know about that. How would we keep you safe?
Now that we know these glasses work, I bet we could make up some special ones for all of them!
Hmmm... That's *very* interesting...
Dad, please!
Sir, it's your call...
You're right. This burden is mine to bear...
Now I know how Atlas must feel...
Daughter, she cannot simply get away with what she and her sisters have done...
She *must* be punished.

Back in New Jersey, they give out community service for some crimes.
Give Medusa community service!
What an *interesting* concept! You mean that we can *make* her do work around the city? For *free?*
Yeah! For a certain number of hours that you'll decide.
I accept this offer, daughter.
We'll put Medusa to work in Mt. Olympus.
Only *once* she has new protective eyewear made.
Dad, this is *so* great! Thank you *so* much. You won't regret this.

So...I can stay with my sisters?
Yeah! Although we may need to find you a new place to live. This place looks a little, uh, rundown...
No need for that, daughter.
Once we have these community hours sorted, I think the first order of business will be to help restore a Mt. Olympus landmark...
The lighthouse!
I'll arrange to have some workers assist.
Would it be okay if I helped too?
I think that would be very good, daughter.

So, people are going to come hang out with me at the lighthouse?
And help fix our home?!
Yes, young lady. That is the plan...although we're going to have a lot of work on our hands.
This place is a real fixer-upper...
We can make it so that your sisters become the primary caretakers of you and the lighthouse.
This is the *best day ever!*
Dial down the enthusiasm... We just found a bunch of bodies in your garage.
Community service? With other people?! This is the *worst day ever!*
That's... slightly better.

Thanks, Dad...
!!
You're welcome, daughter.
Although this was *very* nerve-racking. Please be careful if you're going to take dangerous matters into your own hands!
No promises there.
How did your mother deal with all of this?
With lots of love and patience.
Thank you *so* much.

We'll still need everyone to give a statement...
And we need to ID the statues until we can help them.
We can do that.
This day has been absolutely *bananas*...
At least we know for sure that it wasn't you turning people to stone.
We cleared my name!
Thanks for all your help...
You put yourselves in danger, and Pol—
Pol is going to be fine. If Tina thinks she can fix him, I trust her.
I can...
We're friends. Friends help each other out!

Wanna get out of here?
I think my dad and everyone are gonna be a while...
Yes! Can we?!
I'm gonna stay behind and help a bit.
You sure?
Oh, yeah. You guys go on ahead—I'll catch up with you later.
Want to go to Ambrosia?
YEAH!

We're going to get some food. Okay, Dad?
Let us know if you need anything more.
Okay, honey bear.
Hey, Medusa?
Yeah?
Wanna come to Ambrosia with us?
REALLY?!
Can I go?!
We have to finish giving our statements and—
We're done for now. She can go...
...provided she keeps the protective eyewear on at all times.

Yessssssssssss!
C'mon...I'll introduce you to everyone.
Hey! Medusa's gonna join us!

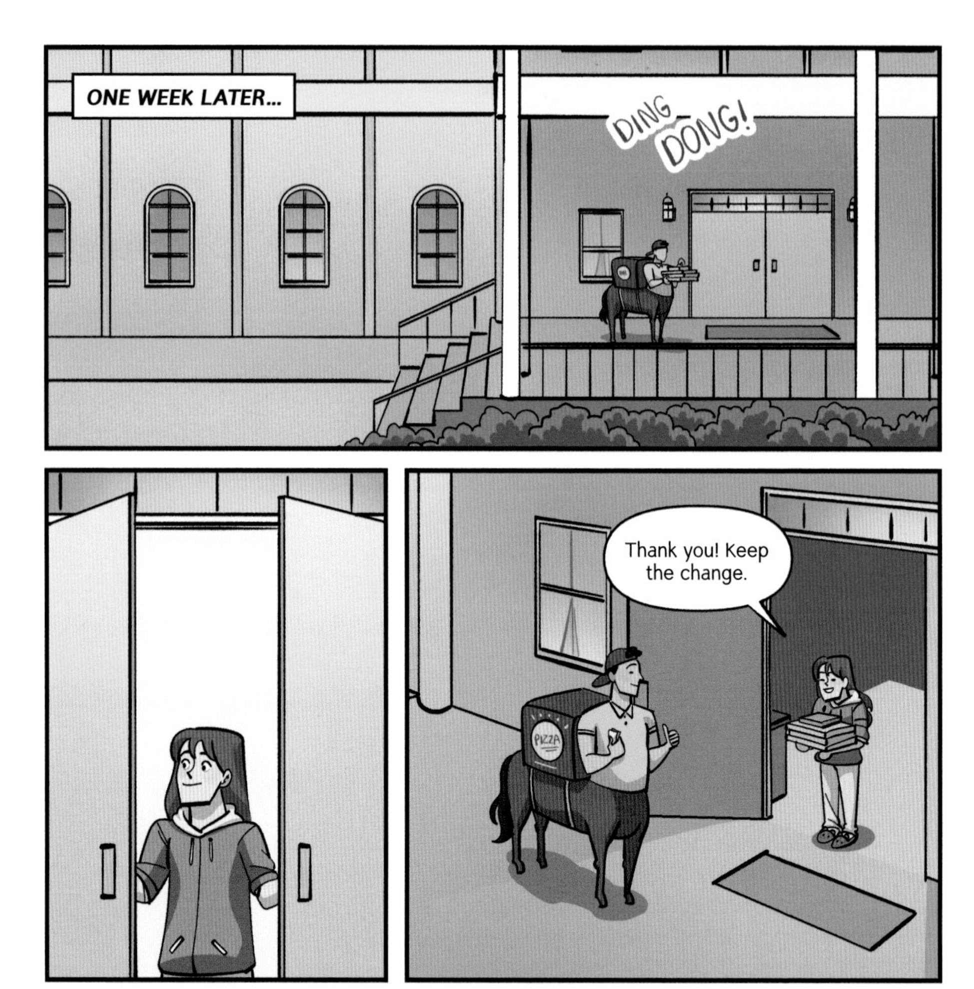
ONE WEEK LATER...
DING DONG!
PIZZA
Thank you! Keep the change.

DAAAAD! PIZZA'S HERE!

IT'S PIZZA TIME!
You *really* love pizza, Dad.
It's *glorious!*
PIZZA

Daughter...
What's up?
I am really happy that you're here.
I know it's been a lot to adjust to, but I want this to work.
I want you to be happy here.
It's *definitely* been a lot, but now it's getting kind of... normal somehow.
I'm happy I'm here too.
I know you're probably confused about me, and Mt. Olympus, and your potential powers, but we'll figure it out together. Okay?
Thanks, Dad. I'd like that.
BZZ BZZ

Hang on, daughter. I'm being paged! It might be important...
Paged? You're being *paged?!*
That is so retro...
I gotta introduce these people to smartphones.
I have to check in. I might be a little bit.
That's okay, Dad. I'm supposed to be playing *HØLØHŪNTĒR*, and my friends are coming by in a bit for a movie.
Okey doke!
ZZA
PIZZA

KAREN'S
ROOM

THERE SHE IS!
Sorry I'm late! I can't play for too long tonight.
We've been waiting on you for five minutes!
Like you can't wait a whole five minutes...
Listen here. Don't think I'm scared of you. I'll smite you in battle!
OOOOOH, I'M SHAKING.
Guys, come on, stop!
What's good, Karenator? How is it there? We miss you.
I miss you guys too. It's real weird here, but it's all right.
It's different from home. Like, a *lot* different.

How's it been with your dad?
That's gotta be awkward, right?
It's been good. He's been trying.
I still feel like I don't really know him, though.
But...he's actually pretty cool so far.
IS HE SPOILING YOU?!
What did we tell you about the mic?!
Oh! Sorry—is he spoiling you?
What does he do?
Are you being well fed?
You know how your mum worries about that.
You ask the dumbest questions. Of course she's being well fed!
No one asked you, princess!

Have you made any new friends?
Yeah— they're just as strange as this place.
But they're really cool. Not as cool as you guys, but getting there.
Any cuties on the horizon?
How are you the worst all the time?!
IT WAS JUST A QUESTION.
LET HER LIVE.
Shut up!
I wanna hear about the cuties!
GUYS. GUYS. GUYS.
I love you. I really do. But I've had a real weird couple of weeks.
I'll answer all your questions and concerns later.
For right now... I just wanna play. Please?

YEAH!
I miss beating you all!
Oh, you're going down, dude.
You too, Rachael!
BRING IT ON, PRINCESS.
Be kind, guys. Be kind.
DAAAAAAAAAAAAAUGHTER!!!
Hang on a sec—my dad is calling me.
Your friends are here!
I gotta run, everyone.
NOOOOOOOOOOOOOO! We're in the middle of a match.
Shut up—she has to go! Don't forget to eat.
PAUSED
LOAD GAME
SETTINGS
OPTIONS
NETWORK
▸EXIT G
Get your first kiss!
Avery, stop it. Love you, Karenator.
LOVE YOU ALL!

HEEEEEY!
POL!!!!!!
It's *so* good to see you.
I guess your plan worked?
Yeah! Dr. Hippocrates helped us out with turning everyone back.
And Officer Soter is *super* happy. The Higher Authorities' crime clearance rate shot *way* up after they solved all those missing-pet cases.

C'mon back!
If you're hungry, we have some pizza and cheesy bread.
HECK YES!
I'm really glad you're all here.
We are too. It's gonna be fun.
It's too bad Medusa couldn't come over too.
I'm sure we'll see her soon. My dad said she enrolled at school!
Maybe she'll need a tutor!
She'll *definitely* need a tutor.
PIZZA
What are we going to watch?
You can pick from any of these!
I'm stoked to just have a nice, *normal* night.

Oh. My. Gods.
I really hope things stay normal for a *while* now...
You mean *normal for Mt. Olympus.*
Well, *yeah!*

AUTHORIZED PERSONNEL ONLY

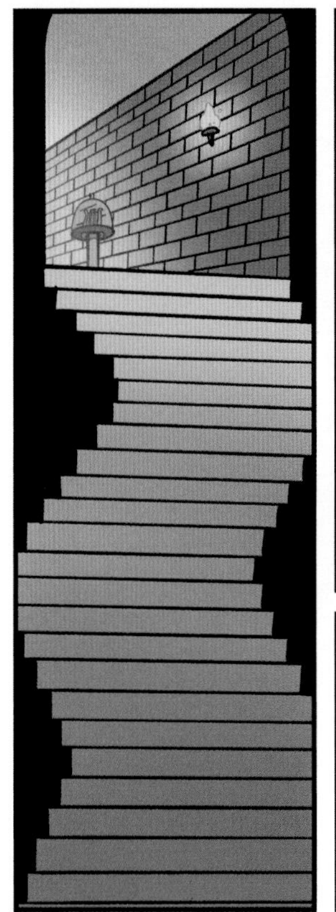

H-h-hello?

WHO GOES THERE?!
I'm Jeff? And umm, I'm really lost...
ARE YOU PREPARED TO ENTER?
Enter what?
Is that the way out?

It is *a* way out...
But many enter and are never seen again...
This will be a test of your resolve.
Are there... snacks?
I've been wandering around down here looking for the exit for a really long time now...
THERE ARE NO SNACKS!
Yikes—okayokayokay...
What *is* this, anyways?
WELCOME TO THE MINOTAUR'S MAZE!
THE END...FOR NOW

KAREN'S MYTHOLOGY NOTES!!!

APOLLO

Apollo is the god of the sun, but also the god of music, poetry, light, enlightenment, healing, plague, and disease. He is the son of the Titaness Leto and the twin brother of Artemis, the goddess of the moon. Apollo is known for being handsome, helping mortals, and protecting them from evil. He participated in many musical contests with other gods, such as Pan, the god of shepherds and sheep, and a satyr named Marsyas.

Did Pol write this, because LOL, I'm never letting him live this down. I guess it's not the worst thing to be known for, and it is true...

ARTEMIS

Goddess of the moon and goddess of the hunt, Artemis is well known for her hunting skills as well as her love of archery and wild animals. She is the daughter of the Titaness Leto and the twin sister of Apollo, the god of the sun. Artemis spends most of her time in the forest roaming around with animals and nymphs and is one of the most respected goddesses.

Got it—remind me to never get on Artemis's bad side... again. I should talk to her about helping me with my archery, though.

NOTE TO SELF:
Text Artemis later.

APHRODITE

Aphrodite is the goddess of love and beauty and was born from the foam of the sea on the island of Cyprus. She is the most beautiful among the goddesses, usually with long, flowing hair and sweet-smelling clothes. The goddess spreads love among women and men, gods and mortals.

Everything here tracks! Dita is an actual treasure... How can you meet her and not immediately feel the love that she radiates?!

Talk about girl crush...